Sita Brahmachari

BRACE MOUTH, FALSE TEETH

Barrington  Stoke

First published in 2014 in Great Britain by
Barrington Stoke Ltd
18 Walker Street, Edinburgh, EH3 7LP

www.barringtonstoke.co.uk

Reprinted 2015

Text © 2014 Sita Brahmachari
Images © shutterstock.com

A CIP catalogue record for this book is available
from the British Library upon request

ISBN: 978-1-78112-400-0

Printed in China by Leo

In memory of Cathy Woodman, whose story about a nursing home and lost false teeth inspired this tale.

Cathy is deeply missed, but her spirit of kindness and compassion lives on.

WORK EXPERIENCE DIARY

BY ZENI CARTER

✤ ✤ ✤ ✤ ✤ ✤ ✤ ✤ ✤ ✤ ✤ ✤ ✤ ✤ ✤ ✤

Alice in Wonderland inspired me to write this.

That's what we call poor old Alice because she does live in her own little Wonderland almost all the time. You know the story – Alice falls down a rabbit hole and has all sorts of adventures. But for my Alice it's a bit different. She falls down a memory hole.

Alice has dementia. She forgets where she is, who she is, and who everyone else is too. She can't even remember the people she sees every day. But I prefer to say that Alice is 'in Wonderland', because 'dementia' sounds like a 'dementor' – a kind of torturer like in *Harry Potter*.

I met Alice while I was on Work Experience. I suppose that what I'm about to share with you is more about me than Alice. It's a kind of diary of my time at Magnolia Gardens Care Home.

I've decided to call it, 'Brace Mouth, False Teeth'. I'm the 'Brace Mouth', Alice is the 'False Teeth'. Say it fast and it's a tongue twister.

"Brace mouth, false teeth. Brace teeth, false mouth. Brace mouth, teeth, false, brace ..."

Well, you get the picture!

If you wear a brace, you may already have covered this page with a shower of spit. Get used to it! Gross-out or not, bodily fluids are just one of the things you've got to deal with if you get Work Experience in an old people's home.

I'm going to take you back to the fateful day when I discovered that I, Zeni Carter, age 14, was heading for Magnolia Gardens Care Home for the Elderly.

THE BOTTOM OF THE PILE

I'm sitting in Mr Wood's office after school because I still haven't found anywhere to do Work Experience. I like Mr Wood. He's one of those teachers who always tries to do his best for you. But I can tell that I'm stretching his patience.

Mr Wood says it's getting harder and harder to find businesses who'll take school students for Work Experience. That may be true, but some people in my class are going to really exciting places. Places they want to go.

My friend Amber's working in the stables she goes to for her riding lessons every week. Laura's off to a publisher's because her mum's a writer and she arranged it for her.

A lot of other people have organised things with their parents' work too. But my mum said,

"Darlin', whatever they give you is going to be better than cleanin' houses!" I suppose she's right. I know how to clean already so it's not like I'd learn anything.

Mr Wood sits behind his desk and turns the pages of a big file he has open in front of him.

"So, Zeni, you said on your form that you wanted to work in publishing, journalism or media," he says.

I just put down the first things that came into my head.

I mutter under my breath, "I don't care where I go really."

"Well, Zeni, if you don't care, you can't expect anyone else to either!" Mr Wood says. "But, as we're talking of caring … how about a care home? It's a small, friendly place, very well run – I know the lady who manages it." His fingers trace over a handwritten letter with a pretty logo of a tree at the top. I strain to read the letterhead from where I'm sitting.

It says 'Magnolia Gardens Care Home'.

My heart sinks. I only half listen to Mr Wood go on about my 'kind heart'.

MAGNOLIA GARDENS
CARE HOME

Magnolia Gardens Care Home is the house I pass every day on my way to school. The one with – of course – the magnolia tree outside. I've often wondered who lives there. The only people I've ever seen going in and out are women in clean white uniforms.

In one of my random daydreams I imagined that those women were the perfect clean petals of the magnolia tree.

The magnolia's just coming into bud. I always think it's a shame that it flowers for such a short time when it's so beautiful. And then its shell-white petals fall and go all mushy and brown. Last year I nearly broke my neck slipping over on them in the rain.

Sorry! My mind's wandered. Where was I? Oh yes – STILL sitting in Mr Wood's office.

"Well, Zeni, you're going to have to decide," Mr Wood prompts.

And that is how I ended up stepping into Alice's Wonderland.

BRACE FITTING

Before Work Experience started I had my brace fitted. Pretty much half our class has had braces at some time, so I didn't think it would be a big deal. I'm quite late with all this brace business, because my second teeth took such a long time to appear. I was hoping for an invisible brace like the one that Laura had, but it turned out that my kind of higgledy-piggledy teeth need a double row of train tracks!

I lay in the orthodontist's chair and listened to her going on about how to clean my brace with these little sticks that look like tiny chimney-sweep brushes with yellow plastic ends. As I left she informed me that I would probably be 16 when these braces came off.

And now my head hurts, my jaw hurts and my teeth hurt like someone's punched me in the mouth.

I've gone through three days of school without opening my mouth to anyone – except Laura and Amber.

I feel as if my lips are sticking out like a fish-pout from the rest of my face and I can't talk properly without spraying everyone with spit.

THE NIGHT BEFORE
WORK EXPERIENCE

My sister Neema switches off her music and rolls over. "Good night," she calls from the top bunk. "You're going to need your beauty sleep for those old dears. You must be dying to go there!"

Within minutes I hear her breath change as she falls asleep. You notice stuff like this when you've shared a room with someone all your life.

I lie awake thinking. A whole week in an old people's home feels more like punishment than Work Experience. How am I going to get on with other people's grandads and grandmas when

I find it hard enough to talk to people my own age? I don't even know any old people. Mum had Neema and me when she was quite young and my gran looks the same age as some of the mums at school. The few old people that I have met have been bossy and grumpy or ... worse.

Mum says in her experience if people aren't nice to you, you shouldn't always assume that they're being racist. People are always trying to work out where Mum's from and it doesn't seem to bother her. But sometimes it's hard not to take offence. Me, Neema and Mum have all felt it – that 'go-back-to-where-you-came-from' look that feels like a punch in your gut.

MONDAY

I don't know what time I fell asleep but in the morning I feel like I've only had about an hour's rest. I get out of bed, swish the curtains back and read my Work Experience letter over again, for the 100th time.

Report to your supervisor

Mrs Netti Hammond, Magnolia Gardens Care Home, Bath Road

On: 24th February

At: 9 a.m.

Other info: Please wear smart but practical clothes.

Laura said 'smart' means anything except jeans or trackies. But that's just about all I own!

I shove the letter in my bag and start to pull clothes out of my wardrobe. In the end I go for black leggings, a sleeveless T-shirt, a zip-up-the-front sea-green sweatshirt, stripy socks (I nicked these off Neema) and my newish purple Vans.

"How do I look?" I make the mistake of asking Neema. She gives me the once-over.

"How are you supposed to look?" she asks.

"Smart but practical," I say.

"Well, you've got about half of that right," Neema laughs. Then she gives me one of her big bear hugs. "You'll be all right, sis. Cos you're wearing my lucky socks!"

I glance down at the note on the kitchen table as I eat my breakfast.

Good luck on your first day!
See you tonight.

Love, Mum x

I put the note in my pocket and head off. As I walk, I imagine that I have never been down this street. I feel as if I'm seeing everything for the first time.

In one garden someone has a collection of stone cats that I've never noticed before. There are small cats, big cats, painted cats and grey concrete cats. Just then I hear a meow and a real black cat disappears into the garden.

Maybe it's good luck! A black cat crossing my path, and all that.

But then I shove my hands in my coat pockets and a crisp packet falls out on to the pavement. An old lady appears and throws some rubbish in her wheelie bin. I'm about to bend down and pick the crisp packet up, when she goes off on one.

"That's the problem with you young people, no respect!" she scolds.

"I was picking it up," I tell her. My voice sounds weird even to myself. I can't quite get my tongue around the words and the spittle gathers behind my bottom brace.

"Likely story," the old woman chunters as she makes her way back to her front door.

'No wonder old people are lonely,' I think.

I go from a black cat crossing my path, to being insulted by an old woman, in a matter of seconds.

Is that good luck or a bad omen?

Now I'm standing outside Magnolia Gardens Care Home. The doorway has white pillars that seem too grand for the size of the house.

I look up through the magnolia tree. Its branches fan out and curl at the ends, like a drawing in a picture book. I reach out to touch the smooth petals that are just unfolding.

"Can I help you?" A rich voice comes from behind my back. I turn and an elegant African woman in a purple head-wrap is peering down at me.

"I like those shoes," the woman says. "My favourite colour, purple! Though some people say it's the colour of madness!" She laughs. I can see she's just being friendly but I already feel purple-hot with embarrassment and can't say a word.

The woman doesn't seem fazed. She smells of cinnamon and oranges. I think it's the same hand cream my mum uses. It's weird but that smell makes me feel a bit better.

"You must be Zenani. I'm Netti," she says. "Where are you from?"

"I live just up the road," I answer, with a sigh of relief when I hear the words flow free-ish around my brace.

"I meant your family," Netti says, patting my arm. "Zenani is an African name, isn't it?"

"Yes," I say. It was my dad's choice, apparently.

I don't tell her that I have no memory of my dad other than as a face in a few photos. In fact, I've only got one of him and me – him holding baby me. I can't feel sad, like Mum and Neema do, because I don't remember him.

"I'm from Nigeria!" Netti smiles at me as if this news has brought us closer.

I say nothing.

"Well, I call this the global house," Netti announces. "Between the staff and the residents of our little care home we span half of the world." She opens her arms wide. "Don't look so worried," she says. "I've got a young man from another school on Work Experience too, so you won't be on your own. I think he's here so he can spend some time with his grandad who's just moved in."

I feel my face burn up in embarrassment. One of the few things I liked about this whole Work Experience was the fact that nobody my age would be around to make me uncomfortable. I feel my hand float up to my mouth and cover it. Is this what's going to happen to me every time I have to do something new? Will I always go back to being the shy, can't-get-a-word-out little girl I thought I had left behind?

"Well, Zenani Carter, let's get to work!" Netti places a comforting hand on my shoulder.

"People call me Zeni," I stutter.

Netti bends down and picks up a single fallen bud from the magnolia tree. "These are like rare butterflies, ready to push their way out from a chrysalis, I always think." She smiles a warm, wide smile at me, then shivers. "We can't hang around out here in the cold all day."

Netti climbs the steps of the grand porch. There's a gold plate above the door with a magnolia flower engraved on it. Netti takes a large keyring from her bag and opens the dark green door. It squeaks as if it's in pain.

"Even the door's getting old," Netti says. "Oiling it can be a job for one of you."

As I step inside the care home, I think, 'I won't last one day in this place, never mind a week.'

The first thing that hits me is the smell. It's something like … Let me work it out … Domestos, cabbage, perfume, washing powder, coffee and un-flushed toilets.

And this all mixes with Netti's orange-cinnamon smell and the too-sweet scent of white lilies that wafts from a vase by the staircase.

The combination makes me sneeze.

"Bless you!" Netti says as she locks the door behind her.

"Thank you," I reply, but I don't feel blessed.

She signs a visitors' book and asks me to do the same. "Make sure you sign in and out every day," she instructs me.

'No one's going anywhere if you have to lock them in,' I think.

It's almost as if Netti has read my mind. "It's a shame we have to lock the door," she says. "But some of our residents get confused from time to time and go for a wander."

She leads me through a panelled hallway, past a staircase with dark wood banisters and navy blue carpet. There's some kind of bird, like a gnarly old hawk, carved on the sturdy bottom pillar. Netti pats it as she passes. "Her beak's worse than her bite!" she jokes.

Just then, a woman comes shooting past.

"Everything all right, Sula?" Netti asks.

Sula's wearing a white nurse's uniform.

"Not to wolly – incident." Sula's voice is high pitched and she delivers the words fast like a chirpy little bird. She nods and gives a dramatic wink as she scurries into what looks like a living room, and through an archway that leads to a kitchen. She opens a cupboard and takes out some gloves, detergent and a bin liner.

"Not to worry!" Netti laughs.

Sula ignores her correction. "Alice say she needing help with teeth again." Sula taps her own teeth. "Still not happy. She say she is wearing wrong teeth, false teeth don't fit."

"Not that again," Netti sighs. "Poor old Alice. She's getting more and more confused every day. I've made her a dentist's appointment for next week. I can't see anything wrong but I just want to make sure …"

Sula wrinkles up her forehead. "No more early appointment?" she asks.

Netti shakes her head. "They asked if it was an emergency, and I couldn't lie and say it was."

"Maybe emergency in Alice mind," Sula says, and taps her own head.

Netti nods in agreement. "If only Alice had some family to anchor her down," she says.

Sula tuts and goes to deal with the 'incident'.

'Great!' I think. First a toilet accident and now this thing about false teeth. I was right. This place is a nightmare. A total nightmare.

Netti and I sit at the big table in the residents' sitting room.

"So this is a list of tasks that you and Joe can share between you," Netti says. She passes over a sheet of instructions. "On top of the everyday jobs, we would like you to offer an activity to one or more of our residents. Something stimulating ..."

All I can think is how embarrassing it's going to be to work with Joe – even though I've not even met him yet. What if I can't get my words out, or worse still, what if I spit on him when I talk?

"Netti!" Sula calls. "Alice weeping for teeth again!"

"Excuse me a moment," Netti says. "Read the sheet. And if any of our residents come into the sitting room, say hello, introduce yourself, and take the time to get to know them a bit. Sula and I are never far away."

'Please don't let anyone walk in – especially not the Work Experience boy,' I think as I pick up the list and attempt to look busy.

You can be of help by:

1. Wiping down chairs and furniture.

2. Offering residents coffee and tea.

3. Making sure water jugs are filled + pouring and offering water.

4. Assisting with serving at mealtimes + if supervised, helping with feeding residents.

Please be aware that you are only allowed to be with residents in common areas if supervised or given permission by a member of staff.

You can improve the quality of life of our residents by:

1. Chatting to them and trying to find out one or two things about each of them.

2. Making a special connection with one of the residents then doing something for them that will really make a difference to their quality of life. Make this your project for the next week.

'Quality of life.' I've heard that phrase before, but I've never really thought about what it means.

Just then a man shuffles into the room on a metal walking frame. He looks at the floor as he concentrates on taking one step after another until he reaches one of the tall-backed chairs and eases himself into it. I don't think he's seen me. I'm just wondering how I can say hello to him without giving him a shock, when he picks up a TV remote with his shaky hand. The news comes on really loud. Then his eyelids grow heavy and his head nods backwards. A sliver of saliva runs down from his mouth across his cheek. Gross! What sort of quality of life is that?

Just then a boy about my age walks in and sits down next to me. "I'm Joe," he says.

His voice is sort of soft, with a smile in it. My face boils up. I can't even see what he looks like because I'm too embarrassed to meet his gaze. Out of the corner of my eye I can just about make out close-shaved hair and dark eyes. Our skin is the same rich brown tone. He's wearing one of those tags on his wrist – the kind you get at a music festival.

"I'm Z– Z–" I can't believe this. "Zeni," I manage to splutter at last, along with a fine spray of spit that showers the table and a bit of his hand. The SHAME of it! My own hand shoots up to my mouth.

Joe smiles and exposes a double row of braces. He slips his hand under the table. I bet he's wiping it on his jeans.

Luckily Netti comes in just then. "I see you two have met. Well! What do you think of our little household?"

"I think Grandpops will like it when he gets used to not being at home," Joe says.

"I'm sure that you will help him settle in this week. You have my permission to spend as much time as you like with him." Netti pats her chest and it squidges like a soft pillow. "This is what I call 'heart-work'," she says. "There are no City salaries, or swanky cars or posh houses … It's hard work, but if you pour just a little bit of your heart into it, you find that the love comes back at you and takes you by surprise." Her eyes glaze over with a kind of passion.

I'm happy for her that she does work that she loves. But I'm struggling to see what I could love about this job.

"If you take the time to find out, you'll be really interested in the lives our residents have had," Netti goes on. "Take your grandad, Joe – he seems like he's had a very full life. A music producer, wasn't he?"

Joe nods.

Netti looks at the sleeping old man in the chair, and goes over to turn the volume on the TV down. While she's at it, she tunes it to Jazz FM.

"Mr O'Connor here likes a bit of jazz," she says. "He's played sax all his life. I'm told his band was a regular at Ronnie Scott's right from when it first opened in the 1950s. Your grandad and Mr O'Connor would have a lot in common."

Me and Joe glance at the old man and I can tell from the brief look between us that we're both struggling to imagine him as a sax player.

"I play a bit of sax, too," Joe says.

"Then you can bring it in and play for him, and your grandad, too," Netti says.

Joe shrugs. "I'm not that good. And it's not easy to play with this thing in!" He points to his brace and glances at me. I wonder if he threw that in for my benefit.

It's stupid, but the fact that he's got a brace too and the way he didn't make a big deal of the spit on his hand makes me think we're going to get on OK.

The phone rings and Netti hurries away to answer it. 'Think of something to say,' I tell myself, but I can't.

"Well, I'm off to spend a bit of time with Grandpops," Joe says. "If I tell him about Mr O'Connor, I might be able to get him to come out of his room. See you later."

"At least he can hide away in his grandad's room," I say to myself. But I wouldn't blame him if Joe's just looking for an excuse to get away from me and my awkward silences.

As Joe passes the wooden bird on the stairs, I wonder what it would say if it could talk. I stare at it for a moment and imagine it turning its spooky glass eyes on me and reading my thoughts.

"Hi, Grandpops," I hear Joe shout. I wonder if his grandad's a bit deaf.

Sula scurries in and places her hand on my shoulder. "The kitchen in total state!" She pulls me through the archway.

I can't believe how much there is to do. Dirty plates are piled up everywhere. Sula hands me a pair of yellow gloves. 'Like mother, like daughter,' I think. There are some people in my class who would learn something if they had to clean up this kitchen, but I'm not one of them.

I put the gloves on and head for the sink. Sula helps me for a while and then a buzzer sounds inside the pocket of her uniform. She hurries off to deal with whatever needs her attention.

Nearly two hours later the kitchen gleams like an advert for a miracle cleaning product.

"Impressive!" Netti nods as she comes into the kitchen. "But don't think I'm going to let you hide out here all the time. You need to meet everyone and you won't do that in the kitchen."

"We're a friendly little set-up here," she goes on. "I've chosen four residents I'd like you to work with and they're all lovely in their own way. There's three men – Mr Wilson, Mr O'Connor, and Mr Daley who is Joe's grandad. And one woman, Alice Clarke. She's blind and can get quite confused. I wonder if all this toothache business is about Alice missing her friend Janice. Janice moved at Christmas, to be near her son and his family," she explains. "They used to sit together and coo over Alice's canaries. Poor Alice is a bit outnumbered now. Once we've redecorated Janice's old room we'll have space for another female resident."

Netti suddenly seems to remember that she's talking to me. "I'm sorry, Zeni, not things you need to worry yourself with," she says. "Coffee and cake time!" She rolls up her sleeves and ties on an apron that says 'Keep Calm and Put the Kettle On'.

In the living room, three old people are now sitting in their chairs. A woman with soft white hair is nearest to me. This must be Alice of the false teeth. She's dressed in a smart silk dress with a tie belt. Around her neck is a string of crystal beads. Her eyes are closed – I notice a shimmer of green eye shadow on her paper-thin lids. On her knee she has a birdcage with one yellow and one green canary inside. They hop about the cage as if she is conducting them with her hands.

Joe is nowhere to be seen. He must still be upstairs. He's lucky – I wish I had somewhere to hide away. I glance at my watch and I can't believe how slowly time is ticking. This is going to be the longest week of my life.

Apart from Alice and Mr O'Connor – who is still snoring in front of the TV – there's a smart-looking man in a checked shirt whose face is hidden behind a large newspaper. He must be Mr Wilson. He lowers his paper when I ask him what he'd like to drink.

"Thank you, my dear, most kind," he says as I return with a cup of coffee. I nod at him and back away.

As I reverse I bump into Alice.

"I'm sorry!" I say. Quick as a trigger, she grabs hold of my arm and clings on to me.

"Is that you, Janice?" she asks. "Have you come back? Someone's got my teeth. No one believes me, but I'm telling you. It's true. I'm blind, not stupid, and these ..." She lifts her hand to her mouth and taps her teeth with her neat nails. "... These are not mine!"

I have to say her teeth do look quite large in her small mouth. As she won't let go of my hand, I have no choice but to kneel down next to her.

"I'm not Janice," I tell her. "My name's Zeni." I'm not sure if she hears me.

The canaries are perched on a swing in the front of their cage. Every time they swing forward they chirp at me. They are so cute with their tiny little faces – like bird jewels. I know Mum says we've got no room for pets, but two canaries wouldn't take up much room, would they? The green one seems to be talking to me!

Just at this moment, Sula crosses the room, nods and smiles. I think she's trying to encourage me. But now Alice's hands are reaching for my hair. It's the strangest feeling, her bony old hands moving over my thick waves.

"Pretty Zeni!" she says.

I keep my eyes on the canaries.

"What colour ... blonde, brown?" she asks.

"Black," I answer.

Now she runs her hands over my cheeks.

"What colour's your skin?" she asks. "White, peach, olive, caramel, mahogany, ebony?"

At first I think she's making a joke, but the expression on her face doesn't change.

"I don't know," I say. I've never been asked to describe the exact colour of my skin before. "Golden brown like caramel, I suppose?"

"Difficult to get a good foundation match, I'll bet," she says. "I keep telling Mr Sugar he should be investing in foundation for all skin colours. But will he listen to me? No, I'm just a silly shop girl!"

I wonder what on earth she's talking about.

"Good bone structure!" she declares.

Now her hands are running over my lips. I want to pull away, but I'm worried it might seem unkind. It's like she's trying to paint a picture of me through her hands. My mouth is open and she feels the front of my braces. My neck stiffens. I can't believe I'm letting her do this.

"Brace mouth?" she asks.

"Yes," I say, with a deep breath. "I've just had it fitted."

"Does it hurt?" she asks, taking my hand in hers.

"It does," I admit. No one's asked me that before.

"Mine too!" She sighs and taps her own teeth again. Then a strange noise emerges from her mouth, like a bell tinkling around the room.

The newspaper man lowers his paper.

"I haven't heard Alice's laugh in a long time!" He smiles at me as if I've done something to make her happy.

Now Alice's laugh is replaced by a little chant. At first I can't make out what she's saying. Then I lean in closer and get it – "Brace mouth, false teeth, false mouth, brace teeth, teeth brace, mouth teeth ... mouse teeth, brace false mouse, mouth ..." As she mixes up the words her own spit showers over me and she bursts into laughter again.

I suppose all the stress of this Work Experience has been building up inside me, ready to explode. It could have come out in tears. But this Alice and her 'Brace mouth, false teeth' chant makes it pour out like a lava flow of laughter. I clutch my stomach as the laughter makes my ribs creak. My chest feels like it's going to burst open. Tears stream down my cheeks. I keep trying to catch my breath, but then the laughter rumbles up and I'm off again! I'm just getting hold of myself when Mr O'Connor jolts awake in his seat.

"What's the crack?" he asks as he looks at the scene of uncontrollable laughter. Mr Wilson's deep bass laugh is booming out and even Netti and Sula are doubled over now.

"Trust me to sleep through the party!" Mr O'Connor smiles at me as I get a grip at last.

I turn to see Joe in the doorway with a man and a woman behind him. I suppose they're his mum and dad. They look a bit taken aback at the scene in front of them.

Netti walks over and shakes their hands.

"I hope Dennis is settling in all right," she says. "Perhaps he'll come and join us in the sitting room soon."

"Seems like a laugh in here!" Joe's dad says. "In the old days Dad would have been in here like a shot. Always sniffing out a party."

Joe's mum wraps her arm around his shoulders. He seems upset.

"Do you mind if we take Joe home now?" she asks. "I know it's a bit early, but ..."

"No, you get off." Netti smiles and pats Joe on the back. "Don't worry. We'll take good care of your grandad. Just give him a bit of time!"

Joe half smiles at me as Netti unlocks the door. His braces glint. He probably thinks that I'm a complete nutter. First the blushing, then the spit and now the over the top laughter.

"Where's Brace Mouth?" Alice asks, holding her hands out towards me. I walk back to her. Someone has placed her birdcage on the floor.

"Where are my darlings?" Alice asks and her hand searches the air.

"Right here next to you," I tell her and I place her hand on the top of the cage. "What are their names?" I ask.

Alice sits up taller in her chair. "Emerald and Sunshine."

"Lovely," I say.

"I'm just happy I got to see them before I lost my sight altogether," Alice says. "Emerald and Sunshine," she repeats. "Pretty names for my darlings. When I say their names I see their colours. Lucky birds, always beautiful. You can't see them getting older, you know." She rubs her fingers together near the cage and the birds begin to sing as if to say thank you for the compliment. Alice tilts her head to the side and listens.

"Will you help me drink my tea?" Alice asks me. A pained look crosses her face. "It's hard with the wrong teeth in."

I can still feel the pressure of my brace against my own teeth. Alice may be confused, but I do feel sorry for her. It's horrible, this feeling that something's not right in your mouth.

It takes me a long time to spoon the tea into Alice's mouth. When she's finished she leans back in her chair with a contented sigh and falls asleep. A little bit of tea runs down her chin, so I take a napkin and dab it away. She's wearing a light-smelling perfume that reminds me of Mum's favourite flowers – sweet peas. Her neat hands are crossed on her knees. She's wearing a plain gold wedding band, with a little diamond ring beside it. It's touching how well she takes care of herself.

I feel a hand on my shoulder and I turn around. Netti smiles down at me. "Well, Zeni Carter, you have brought a little joy to our home on your very first day of work," she says. "I haven't seen Alice this happy in ages. I think we might have struck gold with you!"

As I walk past the magnolia tree, a single white petal wafts towards me.

When I get home, Mum and Neema are sitting at the kitchen table. Mum already has tea laid out for us. It's fish finger sandwiches and cut carrots, apples and grapes. I tuck in – I struggle a bit with the carrots but I manage somehow – I'm really hungry. I was so busy helping everyone that I hardly ate any of the pie we served up for lunch. Anyway, I hate eating in front of people with this brace in my mouth. I can feel Mum and Neema's eyes on me now.

"What?" I ask.

"How was your first day of work?" Mum asks.

"Not too bad," I say.

Later that evening, I lie in bed and feel my eyes grow heavy. I'm never this tired after school. Helping out old people is hard work. As I think this I hear Alice's laughter light up the room and I smile because I KNOW I made Alice happy, just for a moment. I wonder … is this the feeling you get from 'heart-work'?

♡ ♡ ♡

TUESDAY

"Hi, Zeni!"

It's Joe's cheery voice. He sprints up the road towards me, carrying something in a big flat case on his back.

"I thought I better bring my sax in," he grins. He doesn't seem at all bothered about showing off his brace. "I can't have you getting all the glory. Anyway, this is my cunning plan to lure Grandpops out of his room," he says. "If I play to the others there's no way he'll want to be left out."

41

Sula unlocks the door and lets us in. She spots the sax case on Joe's back straight away. "You play music – good idea!"

I don't know what I was expecting when I walked into the sitting room. A fanfare? Alice to jump up from her chair and dance around the room with me? It doesn't happen. When I walk in, she has her head bowed. I touch her on the arm. She grabs me and asks me if I'm Janice, but when I tell her I'm Zeni she pushes me away and refuses to speak to me. I can't tell you how sad it makes me feel that she doesn't want to know me today.

"Don't take offence," Mr Wilson says. "I think she's having one of her 'Lost in Wonderland' days."

Joe and me make tea for everyone and hand it out. Mr Wilson says the same thing every time – "Most kind of you, my dear!" The way he talks I get the feeling he's used to being waited on.

Mr O'Connor's different though – a bit more chilled. He asks me to call him Frankie.

"You set old Alice off yesterday," he says. I like his Irish accent. He sounds like he's singing even when he's talking. "Alice was singin' away all night," he tells me. "Atrocious voice though, to be sure. She should leave the singing to her birds, I say!" Frankie nods over to Alice, who is sniffling in her sleep. "She's properly worn herself out." He winks at me. He seems like the kind of person where a joke and a wink are never far away.

Alice wakes up when I bring her tea. I sit down and stroke her face in the hope that she'll recognise me. When she doesn't respond to my name I even whisper, "It's me – Brace Mouth!"

But her hand is limp. I try to feed her spoonfuls of tea but she just lets it dribble down her chin, so I have to wipe it away. It's as if we've never met.

Joe and I stand at the huge stainless steel sink and I wash while he dries. Somehow it's easier to talk to him now that we're both busy cleaning up. I'm upset and he's upset.

"Grandpops didn't even recognise me this morning!" he sighs. "I said I was going to play the sax and he threw his slipper at me and told me to get out of his room. Charming!"

His voice has gone wobbly. I can tell he's upset even though he's trying to make a joke of it.

"I know it's not the same, but it's got to me that Alice doesn't know me this morning," I tell him. "It's a bit weird, but I was looking forward to seeing her."

Joe coughs and clears his throat. "Sometimes I'm in the middle of a normal conversation with Grandpops when it seems like something short-circuits in his mind. This look crosses his face and it's like he's scared. He holds on to my hand and says this weird thing, 'I have to go now, Joe.' As if he can feel himself slipping away, but he can't stop himself."

I hear the break in Joe's voice, and he rushes to the other side of the kitchen. He pretends to look for something in the cupboard so that I won't see he's upset. I don't know what to say to make him feel better, so I make him a cup of tea.

He laughs. "Thank you, my dear. Most kind!" he says, in Mr Wilson's voice. "Seriously though, thanks. Sorry for bending your ear."

After lunch Joe disappears to his grandad's room and Mr Wilson and I watch *Countdown* together. It's a quiz show – you have to make the longest word you can out of random letters. And when this clock starts ticking you panic. If you're me anyway! Mr Wilson does not have the same problem. He beats all the TV contestants and punches the air in triumph.

"You should so go on that programme," I tell him.

"It's just to keep the old brain ticking over," he says, but he looks pleased.

I keep looking over at Alice to see if there's any chance of her coming out of her Wonderland today, but she just sits there all grey and sad. She doesn't even respond to

Emerald and Sunshine, who are chirping happily in their cage on the floor. I pick the cage up and place it on her knee, but she doesn't hold on to it, so I set it back down on the carpet. It's like a light has switched off in Alice's mind.

There's nothing wrong with Mr Wilson's mind. He says it's his body that's given up on him. He's so riddled with arthritis that he can't get around on his own any more.

"Booked myself in here to save the family the bother of it all," he tells me.

I ask Mr Wilson what he did before he retired. He tells me that he was a barrister.

"Did you have to wear one of those curly white wigs?" I ask him.

"Yes, my dear, I'm afraid I did. And jolly silly I looked too!"

Then Mr Wilson's grand-daughter arrives and I make her a cup of tea. I seem to be making a lot of tea! I don't mind, though. It's not like I'm just cleaning up after people. I wonder if Mum could get a job like this. I think she'd be really good working with old people. She's so kind and patient. Well, she has to be, to put up with me and Neema.

I ask Sula if Alice has any visitors coming today.

"No visitors for Alice," Sula says. "Relatives all moved to Canada. Brought her here, all bills paid, and off they go."

Poor Alice, I think. It's like she's been dumped like an unwanted pet.

"It makes me cry sometime," Sula says. "Such a pride lady too."

From upstairs I hear someone playing the sax. It must be Joe – he was being modest because he's really good. The sound is smooth and light. I walk through the archway to the sitting room and see Frankie's face light up. He gestures towards me as if he wants to stand.

I take his arm and help him walk to the stairs. He rests one arm on the bird's head and one on my shoulder. His fingers tap out the beat on the wood. He can hardly walk, but he shifts from one foot to another, in a kind of jig, as Joe plays. The music is bringing his whole body back to life, bit by bit.

The music stops and Joe appears at the top of the stairs. "My playing sent Grandpops to sleep," he says.

"Well, you got Frankie up on his feet," I say, as Joe walks down the stairs with his sax.

"Give us a blast, son!" Frankie says.

I help Frankie to a seat and he sits down and takes a few deep breaths. He runs his fingers over the shiny saxophone as if he's been reunited with an old friend. Then he raises it to his mouth. He plays a few beautiful phrases but then he has to stop. His breath is all caught up as if he's been running a race.

Netti appears at the top of the stairs. She claps, but Frankie sighs and hands the sax back to Joe.

"Not enough breath left in the old lungs!" he says. "It's not true what they say, Netti – 'Where there's a will there's a way.' I've got the will all right." Frankie has to stop again to catch his breath. "Just not the airways."

"How was work today?" Mum asks that night. She does the thumbs up, thumbs middle, thumbs down thing she's been doing since I started school. How can I explain that working at Magnolia Gardens can be thumbs up, thumbs middle and thumbs down all at the same time?

"Fine," I answer.

I can't get Alice out of my mind in bed that night. 'What can I do to improve Alice's quality of life?' I keep thinking. I fall asleep determined to wake up with a plan ...

WEDNESDAY

My plan is this:

1. Turn the sitting room at Magnolia Gardens into a party area.

2. Put things in it belonging to each of the residents that will ignite happy memories.

"Slow down a bit!" Joe laughs when I tell him. We're in our usual place at the sink, washing up. "On Monday I thought you weren't going to talk to me all week. Now I can't get a word in edgeways!"

I laugh too. "Sorry!" I say. "But what do you think? Is it a good plan?"

Joe lets the dirty water drain out of the sink and starts filling it up again. He pours some washing-up liquid into the bowl and froths it up, then he blows into the sink and a trail of foam bubbles floats across the room. For some reason they make me feel hopeful.

"I was struggling to think of what to do for that 'make a difference' project that Netti keeps going on about," he says. "So maybe your 'Retro Party' idea's the answer."

'Retro Party' – I like the sound of that! Giving the plan a name makes it seem more likely to happen.

Netti is trawling through a list of bills. "Sorry I haven't had more time for you," she says. "I'm all ears now."

She nods as I describe our Retro Party idea. But when I've finished, Netti is more frowning than smiling.

"Have you any idea how much work it'd be to get all that together by Friday?" she asks.

Joe and me nod at the same time.

We must look downcast, because then Netti laughs and her face relaxes into its usual warm expression. "OK," she says. "It's a lovely idea. You can't use the sitting room, but you can deck out Janice's old bedroom. It needs redecorating before anyone else can move in anyway."

Joe and I decide to talk to all the residents, so we can find out about their interests. We start with Mr Wilson. We both get completely absorbed in his story and we're still taking down notes two hours later.

"We'll never get through everyone at this rate," I tell Joe.

Joe offers to talk to his grandad and Frankie, so I can concentrate on Alice. We agree to write everything down, so we can go through it together later.

Sula takes me up to Alice's room. She knocks on the door. There is no answer, but we can hear Alice. It sounds like she's weeping.

We open the door carefully – Alice is propped up on a stack of pillows in bed, wearing a red silk dressing gown.

Sula goes over and strokes Alice's soft white hair.

"Come on, Alice, cheer up," Sula says. "You've got a visitor." Sula goes into the little bathroom and picks up a glass jar. Inside the jar are Alice's teeth, floating in murky blue water. It's so gross. It really does look like a mouth is alive in that glass!

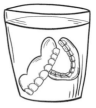

"Put teeth in now, Alice, so you can talk to Zeni," Sula says.

Alice closes her lips tight shut so her wrinkle-lines pucker up and make her mouth look like a shrivelled prune. Then she shakes her head.

Sula raises her hands in defeat. "OK. If you change mind, press buzzer. I'm just outside here cleaning hall," Sula tells me as she picks up some washing and heads for the door.

The weeping sound that Alice is making is like a dog whining. She takes a cotton hankie out of her dressing gown pocket and dabs at her eyes, though I can't see any actual tears.

"Ith that you, Janice?" Alice lisps, and reaches out for my hand. Her voice is sweet and high. It reminds me of her canaries singing. Alice has the cage right next to her on the drawers by her bed. I wonder if Emerald and Sunshine are her closest friends now. She really does seem to miss Janice.

"It's Zeni," I tell her.

"I don't remember that name Zeni," she says. "Are you my daughter?"

I shake my head and then remind myself that she can't see.

"No," I tell her. "Don't you remember me? I'm Brace Mouth!"

Alice's fingers tap lightly on her bed sheets and a smile spreads across her face. She breaks into that strange tinkling laughter, and this seems to bring her memory of me back ... She claps her hands together.

"Brace mouth, false teeth! Brace mouth, false teeth," she chants.

I try not to feel disgusted as she spits at me through her toothless lisp, but I suppose we're well matched. If anyone should understand, I should!

Alice keeps jerking her hand towards the glass with her false teeth. I think maybe she wants to put them in after all and I try to pass the glass to her, but she pushes it away. Some of the water spills on to my leggings. I think I'm actually going to be sick. Then real tears start to roll down Alice's cheeks, and I get over myself.

"Not my teeth. They don't fit me!" she cries. "Brace Mouth, please help me find my teeth. You believe me, Brace Mouth, don't you?" She sits up in bed, all excited, and clasps my hands.

I can hear Sula outside. I wish she'd come back in. It seems mean to argue with Alice so I say, "Yes! I believe you!" and she squeezes my hands even tighter. "I'll ask the others about your real teeth," I promise her.

Beside the birdcage there is a black and white photo of a girl of about 18 or 19, with enormous sparkling eyes. This must be Alice when she was young. I wish I knew what colour

Alice's eyes are – she always has them closed. I could ask her, but I don't want to upset her.

In the photo, Alice has long hair curled in a fancy style, and pinned with flowers. She's wearing a clingy wedding dress and crazy high-heeled shoes. A tall man in a smart black suit stands next to her. He looks older than her. He's grinning at the camera as he holds her arm, like it's the proudest moment of his life. Alice is laughing at the camera. She's really beautiful.

♡♡♡

I pick up the photo and hand it to Alice. "You looked lovely on your wedding day," I tell her. Alice feels around the carved wooden edges of the frame, but her face is blank. I describe the girl in the picture. It's really hard to do.

"You've got a satiny dress, you look like a model ... and you've got flowers in your hair."

"... Satiny ... flowers ..." Alice repeats and then feels her wedding ring on her finger and turns it. "Roses and freesias and jasmine," she says with her toothless lisp.

Alice sniffs the air as if she's back in that day. I look at her bouquet in the photo. I'm not brilliant at flower names, but I do recognise roses in there.

"My Lucas came to buy perfume for his fiancée and fell in love with me," Alice says. "Love at first sight! That's what it was."

I wait for more, but then Alice starts to sing. She's like one of those people on talent shows who are 100% sure that they can sing, even though they seriously can't. She lifts her arms in the air and starts swaying as if she's dancing with someone.

"What was your first dance?" I ask her.

She doesn't answer me. "Why must I be a teenager in love?" she sings. Then she keeps singing and doesn't stop till she gets to the end of the song.

Netti pops her head around the door. "She was crying last time I looked in," she says. "I'm telling you, you've got the heart-work gift, girl!"

Netti pauses for a moment, as if she's making up her mind about something. Then she walks over to the chest of drawers, takes out a book and hands it to me.

"I wouldn't give this to just anyone," Netti says. "Alice's family left it for us. Sometimes we try to use it to talk to her about her past. We haven't had much luck, but you might."

The book's covered in old patterned wallpaper. It's textured so that a bit of the pattern is raised. When you run your fingers over it, it feels like velvet. It's the same red as Alice's dressing gown.

I turn to the first page and see it's a scrapbook. There are black and white photos of Alice in school uniform. There's a ballet dancing certificate and a photo of her and some other dancers on stage. There are model-type pictures too – the kind you see in retro photo shoots. I flick forward. There's a photo of Alice with a newborn baby. Loads of baby and toddler pictures with Alice and Lucas and a little girl. Alice and Lucas and the little girl making sandcastles on a beach.

I feel anger rising up in me. I don't understand how Alice's daughter could leave her here all alone.

I see a close-up picture of Alice looking elegant at what must be her daughter's wedding. Her eyes are still beautiful – their colour is emerald, just like her green canary.

I flick back to the pictures of Alice when she was younger. I stare at a photo of her standing behind a perfume counter, made up and with her hair in an elegant swirl. At the bottom of the photo in looping, old-fashioned writing, it says, 'First day at Selfridges'.

How did Alice say she met her husband? He came to buy perfume for his fiancée and fell in love with her instead.

"What perfume did Lucas buy you, Alice?" I ask.

She raises her wrists to her nose and seems to be breathing in the scent.

"Joy," she says. "Jasmine and rose notes – you can't go wrong with it. It's my personal favourite."

I have the feeling Alice has fallen down a rabbit hole in time and is standing at the perfume counter talking to Lucas, not me.

After work Joe comes round so we can talk about the residents and decide what to get for them to help bring back happy memories.

I have NEVER had a boy back for tea before. Neema and Mum try not to make it into a big deal, but just about everything they do is extra. We don't normally have roast dinner and pudding mid-week.

Netti could only give us a tiny budget, so we'll have to beg or borrow most things for our party, or ask the families for donations. We know we can't get everything on our list, but at least we have a day to collect it all together.

Mum and Neema want to hear about it all. I read out the notes I've made on Mr Wilson – his stories of a lonely childhood as an evacuee in the war. It's hard to think of the grand-looking

Mr Wilson as a little boy standing on a station in his long socks and grey shorts crying. Joe and I both noticed that something happened to his voice when he told his evacuation story ... it sort of quivered. All the 'I-know-what-I'm-talking-about' tone drained out of it.

Neema googles the list of bands Frankie O'Connor's played in and it turns out that he's had gigs just about everywhere. "I'm embarrassed I even tried to play in front of him," Joe groans as we watch an old clip of Frankie O'Connor and his Jazzmen on YouTube.

"You shouldn't be embarrassed," I tell him. "He loved it."

Joe smiles at me, and I smile back. I don't care any more about showing my brace, but I hope Neema didn't catch the look between us. I'll never hear the last of it if she did!

Joe starts telling us about his grandad's schooldays in Jamaica, swimming in the sea, playing the steel pan as a young man, starting his working life as a chef, then meeting Joe's grandma on the ship to England in 1955. He even remembered the name of the ship. The SS *Auriga*.

He tells us that his grandad had struggled to find a place to live. You would not believe the racism in those days. 'No Blacks. No Dogs. No Irish' – that's what they put on the 'Room to Rent' signs.

Joe said he'd heard some of his grandad's stories before, but not all of them. His grandad had never told him the name of the ship he came over on before. "It feels weird to be learning all this when Grandpops is losing his memory," he says. "Do you think it's right for us to bring up the past?"

"You dig up the good bits and the bad bits have to come out too," Mum says, and I know she's not only thinking of Joe's grandad.

Neema and Mum listen as me and Joe discuss what memory-prompts we think we'll be able to get hold of. When they both offer to help I feel that weird warm glow inside again.

Later on, when I'm on my own, I read over the list that we've made:

Memory-Prompts – hopefully photos, if nothing else, for all of them.

Mr Daley (Dennis) – Joe's grandad

Joe will find all of these:

- Old photo albums from home, lots of wedding photos

- Ska and reggae albums and singles (his favourite music is from the film *The Harder They Come*)

- His old record player

- His old football boots

- DVD of England winning the World Cup 1966

- Pictures of Jamaica

- Yucca plant

- Food: Jerk chicken and rice, fried bananas (Joe's dad to help him to make?)

Mr O'Connor (Frankie)

Mr O'Connor's already called his family and some of the Jazzmen from his old band to invite them and to ask them to bring something if they can.

- His favourite saxophone from home (he'd like to start to play a bit again)

- A playlist of songs by him and his band (to download)

- John Coltrane albums (*Blue Train* and *Stardust* sound good. To download)

- Photo album of his childhood in Ireland with all his brothers and sisters (this is in his room)

- Photo of him as a young soldier in his uniform during World War Two

- A VIP press pack of clippings and reviews of his skills as a saxophonist (Joe to make, if time)

- Food: Spicy lamb curry (Sula has offered to cook this)

Mr Wilson (Charles)

Mr Wilson to phone his family to see if anyone's free to come. He'd love to see his dog Bess, if Netti will bend the rules. (But he doesn't want a fuss made.)

- Wedding photo album (this is in his room)

- His barrister's wig (in his room)

- Old broadsheet newspapers from important days in history (Neema to hunt around for these)

- *Private Eye* magazine (we'll buy if time)

- His youngest great-grandchildren

- Food: A plate of fine cheeses (we'll get)

Mrs Clarke (Alice)

I've said I will try to sort these things for Alice.

- Teeth (in her dreams!)

- Perfume bottles (samples – ask Neema to get from Selfridges?) Some of those old-fashioned squirty ones, with the thing you squeeze?

- Joy by Jean Patou – perfume sample

- Make-up (borrow from Mum and Neema?)

- Old pictures of Selfridges to describe to Alice (print off the net)

- Flowers for the table – roses, freesias, jasmine, if we can get hold of them (are they out of season?)

- Music. Especially the song, *Why Can't I Be a Teenager in Love?* (to download)
- Food: Afternoon tea and cakes on a cake stand (Mum to borrow cake stand)

When I go to bed, my mind won't stop racing so I do random things like googling, 'How long does a canary live?' Apparently it's about ten years. If Alice has seen the colour of Emerald and Sunshine, as she said, she can't have been blind for more than ten years. Poor Alice. I wish I hadn't told her that I'd ask the other residents about the teeth. I hope she won't remember asking me.

When I look back at my diary for the beginning of the week I feel a bit ashamed of myself for what I thought and said about these old people before I heard their stories.

THURSDAY

Mr Wilson is the first person I ask about Alice's teeth.

I hand him his morning tea and sit down on the stool next to him. I rehearsed the question all the way up the road and I still can't find the right words. Mr Wilson raises his white bushy eyebrows as if to say 'I'm waiting'.

"It's about Alice's teeth," I mumble. "I hope you're not going to be offended, but I promised her that I would ask every resident in the house if there's any chance that they might be wearing the wrong false teeth."

A strange noise comes out of Mr Wilson's mouth, his face turns beetroot red and his eyeballs pop out. His mouth opens and he splutters bits of biscuit everywhere. He slaps his knee hard and rocks on his seat.

I run to the kitchen and pour a glass of water. By the time I get back, Mr Wilson's cough has turned into laughter and he seems incapable of stopping.

"How come I always miss the jokes?" Frankie asks. "First Alice, now Mr Wilson. I'll be offended if it's not my turn for a belly laugh next!"

Mr Wilson makes an attempt to explain.

"Zeni ... wants to know if ... I'm wearing Alice's teeth!" he manages to get out before he starts laughing again.

At last Mr Parker accepts the glass of water that I hold out to him. "My dear, my teeth are probably one of my most valuable assets." He taps his front teeth and I realise they're his own. "I always tell my grandchildren, 'If you want to be rich, become a dentist,'" he says. "We all want to hang on to our teeth. How about you, O'Connor? Sure you're wearing the right ones?"

Frankie is grinning at me now and I can't help grinning back.

"Get ready for this," Frankie says.

I nod and he throws open his mouth as wide as he can to reveal a mix of missing, filled and gold-capped teeth.

"Not guilty as charged! I rest my case, me lord!" Frankie laughs and doffs a pretend cap at Mr Wilson.

Well, that's it then, because Joe says his grandad is proud of having all his own 'pearly whites'. Well, at least I gave them a laugh and I can tell Alice that I tried.

In the afternoon, Joe and I set to work cleaning out Janice's old room. We take the bed out to make it look like an ordinary room instead of a bedroom. We open the windows and a breeze wafts in. It takes us an hour just to clear the space. Netti comes in with her keys and opens up the bathroom. She has a quick look inside the cabinets.

"We'll have to clear all this out tomorrow," Netti sighs, and locks the door behind her again.

"My mum said she'll help out in the morning if you want," I tell her.

Netti nods. "I never turn down help. Do you think she'd mind cleaning the bathroom? We've been meaning to do it, but there just aren't enough hours in a day."

"No, she won't mind," I say, but I think, 'Poor Mum, as if she doesn't clean enough!'

We spend the rest of the day collecting together memory-prompts and decorating the room. It's time to leave when Mr Wilson's grand-daughter turns up with a van full of things for him – and he said he didn't want any fuss! The room's beginning to look like a proper retro café!

She's hardly been gone for five minutes when Neema rings on the doorbell. She's got two huge bags stuffed full of samples of perfume and make-up.

"What about setting Alice up with her own perfume counter?" Neema suggests. So we drag another table through from the sitting room, put a white tablecloth over it and I begin to lay out the bottles.

"I raced to Selfridges after college," Neema says. "I told the girls behind the counter about

Alice working there in the 1950s and 1960s and they were really interested. The manager told me that the counter girls back then were models too. They used to walk around the store promoting the clothes as well as the make-up. I can't believe they gave me all these samples. I even got the one Alice said was her favourite. They still make it. The manager told me it's a classic."

"I can tell that you're sisters!" Joe whispers to me.

"Most people don't think we look alike," I tell him. It's true, we don't. Neema's inherited more of Dad's looks and I look more like Mum.

"Not the looks!" Joe winks. "The motor-mouth!"

By this time it's about 7 o'clock and the room is looking pretty. Netti comes in and laughs at us.

"If you don't go home soon and have some rest I'll be in trouble for making you work such long hours!" she says.

I don't think I've ever felt so tired. But, so what? I tell myself I can sleep at the weekend.

When I get home, the baking begins!

Mum's borrowed a fancy cake stand, and she has some pretty napkins and cupcake cases. We bake and ice all these little buns. It's been ages since Mum, Neema and me got together to do something like this. We make far too many, but they look lovely when they're all on the cake stand. Alice will love them!

The cake smell is wafting around the flat. I lie in bed sniffing the sweet air and I feel excited like I haven't felt in years, even on Christmas Eve. I can't wait for tomorrow, but at the same time I don't want it to come too soon – I want to savour all the work and, I suppose, care, that's gone into getting ready for the Retro Party day.

FRIDAY

We finish decorating the party room, and then I go to find Alice. She's sitting on her bed in her dressing gown. Emerald and Sunshine are singing happily and Alice is singing back to them, but not as tunefully.

"Hi, Alice," I say.

"Is that you, Brace Mouth?"

"Yes, it's me! Shall I get you ready for the party?" I ask her, feeling all warm inside that she recognised my voice.

"Ooooh, I love a party!" Alice grins with her gummy, empty mouth. I dread her asking about the teeth. I just pray she's forgotten about them.

I get all of Neema's samples of moisturiser and make-up and lay them out. "I'm going to do your make-up," I tell her.

Alice nods, props herself up on her pillows and offers me her face. She must have sat at her counter so many times and put make-up on other people. I want to make this feel as professional as possible. It's a good job Neema let me practise a few times on her.

First, I take the little round pads and clean Alice's skin. Then I squeeze some moisturiser out of a sachet and smooth it over her cheeks and under the paper-thin sacks of her eyes.

Alice sniffs and takes a deep breath. "Lavender and ... bergamot," she says.

I turn the packet over. It's incredible – she's right! I don't even know what bergamot is.

Then I have a look at the little pots of eye-shadow. Poor Alice – her eyes were so sparkly. It's silly of me, but when I finish putting on the eye-shadow I half expect her to open those huge emerald green eyes I saw in all her photos and … see!

I dab a bit of blusher on her cheeks. Then I put some lipstick on her lips.

"What colour?" she asks.

I look at the bottom of the stick. "It says 'Natural Bloom'."

Her tinkling laugh rings out again. "It's like what Lucas calls me – 'Blooming Gorgeous!'" She pulls a gruff face and lowers her voice to pretend – not very well – that she's a man. "What are you doing caking all that muck over your face?" she says. "He's always saying that. I think he's worried in case the other fellas show an interest in me!"

I laugh. It's good to hear Alice say more than just a few words. What's the point in telling her that Lucas died years ago? She's happy.

When I've finished, Alice holds out her hands. It takes me a second to realise what she wants. Perfume. I carefully open the sample bottle that Neema brought and dab some scent behind her ears and on her wrists. She takes a deep breath and inhales.

"Joy! You found my Joy," she whispers.

I wipe the tears from my eyes. I always get a bit emotional when I'm tired, but maybe these tears are to do with Alice. I take a brush and smooth her hair. It's like that angel hair you put on a Christmas tree, or the white feathers that chicks have – thin and soft and fine.

"Sula says she's coming to help you dress," I tell her. "What do you want to wear?"

"Something for the catwalk!" She grins and gets up from the bed.

I open the wardrobe and I can't believe my eyes. There are short dresses, long dresses, blouses, cardigans, shawls, belts, tights, handbags and, at the bottom, shoes of every colour – lots of high heels. On hooks at the side of the wardrobe there are silk scarves, shawls and pashminas in a rainbow of colours.

There is a look of absolute focus on Alice's face as she feels her way through her wardrobe. She seems to remember each item of clothing.

But her hands are restless – she's searching for something in particular.

"What sort of thing are you looking for?" I ask her.

She waves me away as if I'm an interfering shop assistant.

"I'm just browsing!" she tells me. Now she's feeling over a long velvet and taffeta dress with a sparkly clasp at the neck.

"This is the one. Lucas loves me in emerald green! He always says it brings out my eyes."

She takes the dress out of the wardrobe, lays it against her body and twirls her hips this way and that.

"Now for shoes!" she says. "Not too high. The black patent leather or the emerald green ones, I think. You won't believe how sore your feet can get walking around this store all day."

Sula comes in and I go downstairs. The food is mounting up on the kitchen table.

The Retro Party room is as ready as it will ever be, and it looks amazing!

Netti has brought in a rich red rug and it covers almost the whole floor. The room is quite big, so we've divided it into different areas.

The little round tables we found in the garden shed make one end look a bit like a café. Sula has ironed white tablecloths for us. Alice's flowers – roses, freesias and winter jasmine – are dotted around the tables in old jam jars that I found in the kitchen cupboard. And we've made a collage of Joe's grandad's photos of Jamaica. We've put it up behind the tables and it looks great.

The dance floor is at the other end. Frankie's son Freddy is working today, but last night he dropped in Frankie's old record player and albums and we've set up a DJ table. There's an enormous painting of the Courts of Justice leaning against the wall. It belongs to Mr Wilson and he has no idea it's here. It shows an elegant old building with a sunset sky – the kind of painting you see when you go on art gallery trips with school. Mr Wilson's grand-daughter smuggled it in under a blanket, along with a tea set.

In the middle of the room there's a little chest of drawers with the perfume samples laid out. When Netti sees them she looks at me, confused.

"They're for Alice," I explain. "She used to work on the perfume counter at Selfridges."

"Well, I never knew that," Netti says. She dabs a bit of perfume on her wrist and sniffs.

"Do you like it?" I ask.

"No, I don't like it ... I love it!" She laughs and hugs Joe and me to her.

Joe squirms away first. He puts Frankie's music on, and then we invite the guests in.

"I don't believe I've been to this club before!" Frankie jokes. "But someone's got great taste in music."

"I'm just going to see if Grandpops is ready," Joe says. "Maybe I'll tempt him down with the promise of jerk chicken. Wish me luck!"

'Please make him turn up, for Joe's sake,' I think. 'And please make Alice turn up too.'

For me, this whole thing is for Alice. All the other residents have their family around them. She only has me.

Now Mr Wilson is making his way into the room with the help of his walking stick. When he gets to us I'm pouring tea for Frankie from a posh teapot. A grin spreads over Mr Wilson's face as he recognises his china and his painting on the wall.

"Oh my dears, you have excelled yourselves!" he exclaims, and he limps over to the painting. He stands in front of the canvas for a long time.

Now Mr Wilson's grand-daughter and his twin great-grandsons arrive. The twins sit on his knees and a fat Labrador settles by his feet. The dog looks up at him with complete adoration in his eyes. Mr Wilson tucks into his cheese and biscuits. His grand-daughter takes a photo of them all together, and he looks up at her and smiles.

"You know, Grandpa, you can always come and live with us," she says.

"Goodness me, no. Too much commotion for me!" Mr Wilson laughs as one of the twins squirms on his knee. He pats his dog's head and slips him a bit of cracker.

Frankie is having a laugh with two members of his old band, but there is no sign of Alice or Joe's grandad. When Alice comes down I want her to know that I'm here for her – she's not alone. I imagine her standing at the pretend perfume counter and I hope that somehow she'll know I have done this for her, that I've listened to her stories. I so want her to know that I care about her in her Wonderland.

Sula comes in with a sad look on her face. "Alice says tell Brace Mouth she can't come to party, because false teeth don't fit!"

Netti sees the look of disappointment on my face and pats me on the shoulder. "Part of working with the elderly is patience, and respecting their wishes," she says. "Maybe the teeth are her excuse. We can't force her to come."

Joe returns, leading his grandad by the arm. His grandad looks confused. Joe runs over to the record player and changes the record. *"You can get it if you really want,"* the singer blasts out to a funky ska beat.

"Desmond Dekker, Jimmy Cliff … my man!" Suddenly Joe's grandad is smiling.

Joe comes over with a plate of jerk chicken. "See what you think of that, Grandpops!" he says.

His grandad takes a bite and nods his head. He looks up at the pictures of Jamaica on the wall and grins. "Not at all bad!" he says. "Not as good as my Vera used to make, but not bad at all for you, son." He pats Joe on the back.

Just then an enormous yucca plant walks into the room. Joe's dad is hidden behind the rubbery fans of its branches.

Joe's dad hugs his dad. "Joe told me that you wanted this with you," he says. "We didn't realise." He places the plant beside one of the little tables. Joe's grandad sits down next to Frankie and Mr Wilson, Joe introduces them all and they soon get chatting. Joe stands back and watches.

I watch them too. Joe's grandad chats for a while and then bashes Frankie on the back and bursts out laughing.

"Know what I was saying about those hate-filled signs they put up when I first came to this country?" he asks Joe. " 'No blacks. No dogs. No Irish?' "

Joe nods.

"Well, we come a long way since dem days. Looks to me like we all sit round the same table in the end!"

Joe's grandad laughs. Joe laughs too.

I'm pleased. I think Joe sees the party as his chance to help his grandad get to know the other residents. He was worried that when we go back to school next week, his grandad would just sit in his room and get lonely. No chance of that now!

After a while, the people, music and chatter get too much for me. I look over at the perfume bottles and I feel like I've failed Alice.

I slip out of the room and sit on the bottom step of the staircase. The wooden hawk stares down at me. I feel like it's sitting in judgement on me.

Just then Mum and Neema arrive.

Neema narrows her eyes at me. She always knows when I'm upset. We all sit on the bottom stair, Mum with her arm around one side of me, and Neema with her arm around the other. I tell them that I feel like a complete failure because Alice won't come to the party. "She says it's because of her teeth, but that's an excuse – she doesn't want to come," I say.

"What is it about these teeth?" Mum asks.

"She just keeps on and on about the teeth she has not being hers!" I sob.

All of a sudden, Mum jumps off the step, hurries to a store cupboard in the hall and drags out a cardboard box. "I put everything I found while I was cleaning the bathroom in here," she says. She rummages through the box and comes out holding a set of false teeth!

Mum goes to get Netti. Netti goes to get Sula. The three of them are all in a fluster.

"Janice had a new pair fitted, don't you remember?" Netti says. "You know what they were like. They were always giving each other things – swapping this and that from their toilet bags. But teeth? Surely not!"

Sula pulls a face. "No! It's not possible!"

Netti laughs. "It's worth a try," she says.

We all traipse off to Alice's room. She looks amazing in her dress and smart shoes, but she's sitting on her bed looking sad and vacant again. She lifts her head when she hears us coming.

"Brace Mouth, is that you?" she asks.

Neema giggles.

Sula goes into the bathroom to clean the teeth that Mum found.

"Where are my false teeth?" Alice demands.

Netti hands Alice the teeth she's been wearing up till now. She puts them in. "They don't fit!" she says, and stamps her feet. "They are not my teeth!"

Netti holds out her hand for the new teeth.

Sula dries them and passes them over.

"Let's try these for size then, Alice!" Netti says.

Alice slots the teeth into her mouth and a smile dawns on her face.

And then, as we watch, Alice straightens her shoulders and stands up. She looks as if she's ready to model the most expensive, glamorous dress in all of Selfridges. She smiles at us. "Now I'm ready to party!"

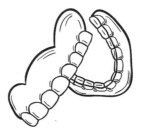

THE WEEK AFTER ...

At school, they asked us to think about what we'd learned during our Work Experience week.

Some people enjoyed theirs. Others found it boring. It helped some people work out what they want to do, and others found out what they don't want to do.

And me? Well, it taught me that when I set my mind to do something I can make it happen. I still don't know what job I want to do, except that I hope it involves some kind of 'heart-work'. I think 'heart-work' is what I'm good at.

I'm not a top-of-the-class person. In fact, I've never won anything at school. But I don't care about that now because I feel like I've made a difference to someone else's life. I've made a lonely old woman happier.

One of the best things to come out of my Work Experience is Mum's new job – one that she actually likes – at Magnolia Gardens! She does a bit of everything – cooking and cleaning and sitting with the residents. She also helps Netti with the accounts.

A new resident, Jessie, has moved into the Retro Party room. Jessie and Alice seem to enjoy sitting together, even though Alice calls her Janice most of the time.

"Girl Power!" Netti calls it.

Many of the memory-prompts have moved to the sitting room now. They will get added to every time there's a new resident. I like the idea of a room that changes as people pass through it.

Hardly a day goes by when me and Joe don't pop into Magnolia Gardens on our way home. It's become our meeting point. Joe's grandad keeps joking with us that we only go there to see each other. I admit, there's a grain of truth in that! It does feel like the place where me and Joe are most at home with each other ... and he did ask me out when we were standing under the magnolia tree.

Joe reckons that his grandad fell in love with Alice at the party, when she sent Emerald and Sunshine down and insisted on making a catwalk entrance into the room herself.

"Oh man, prettiest bird in the house," Joe's grandad said, looking from the canaries to Alice. "If her name's Alice I don't mind being in no Wonderland with she! And she smell like a dream too."

Sometimes Alice calls Joe's grandad 'Lucas' instead of Dennis, but he doesn't put her right – he just takes her hand as they sit together surrounded by their own memories.

The petals of the magnolia tree have all fallen now, and there's been no rain so the garden looks and feels beautiful, like a carpet of velvet petals.